For Sarah Louise

Copyright © Robert Ingpen 1986

First published 1986 by Thomas C. Lothian Pty Ltd,
Melbourne, Australia

This edition first published 1999 by
Happy Cat Books, Bradfield, Essex CO11 2UT

A CIP catalogue record for this book is available
from the British Library

ISBN 1 899248 78 1

Printed in Hong Kong

The Idle Bear

Robert Ingpen

Winner 1986 Hans Christian Andersen Medal

Happy Cat Books

"What kind of a bear are you?" asked Ted.

"I'm an Idle Bear."

"But don't you have a name like me?"

"Yes, but my name is Teddy. All bears like us are called Teddy."

Ted thought for a while, then said, "Well, Teddy, I have been Ted forever— at least fifty years, I think."

"Me too," said Teddy, "at least that long."

We could be related, thought Ted and Teddy together.

"We are related!" announced Ted, pretending he had known for ages.

"How can you tell, Ted?" challenged Teddy, "How do you know?"

"Oh, I just know. Everybody has relations, I think especially where I come from," said Ted beginning to wish it wasn't so.

"Where do you come from, Ted?"

"From an idea," said Ted definitely.

"But ideas are not real, they are only made-up," said Teddy. "You have to come from somewhere real to have realitives."

"Not realitives, relatives!" said Ted trying to hide his confusion.

Ted remembered that everybody he had met had come from 'up the street', and said, "I come from up the street."

"What street?" questioned Teddy.

In desperation Ted said, "Up the street next to your street."

"What happens up the street?"

"That depends," said Ted, now really confused, "That depends on everything else that happens." *That should do*, thought Ted.

"Like what?" demanded Teddy.

Ted tried to remember. "When I was young,"
he began, "I used to have a lot to do.
I was as important as a bear can be,"
Ted paused, then went on,
"later I was put away, and taken out,
and put away, and taken out, and put . . ."

"Put away where?" interrupted Teddy.

"In a box."

"What sort of a box? A bear box?"

"I don't know," said Ted, "just a box."

"Oh," said Teddy.

"Have you got a growl?" said Ted.

"I used to have one but it wore out,"
said Teddy.

"Mine still works," said Ted proudly, "at least
I think it does."

"Don't you know?"

"That depends," said Ted, "that depends on
what I do. If I stand like this it works sometimes.'

Ted stood on his head as best he could.

Then he bent backwards.

"It's something to do with my tummy, but
I've never seen it," Ted said and stood
on his head again.

"It's a very small growl, Ted," said Teddy.

"It's better than a worn out growl," said Ted
feeling challenged again.
"It used to be very loud.
I used to be full of growl
when I was young,
up the street."

"I'm full of straw," announced Teddy.

Ted ignored that. It sounded reasonable and anyhow he was probably full of straw too, if they were related. But then scarecrows and cushions are full of straw and the thought of being related to a cushion annoyed him.

Ted was still thinking about cushions and scarecrows when Teddy startled him by saying, "Dogs."

"What about dogs?" said Ted.

"Dogs come from up the street,"
announced Teddy.

Ted thought, *of course they do,*
and remembered Michael.
He hadn't seen Michael for how long?
"It must be forty years," thought Ted aloud.

"What?" said Teddy.

"It must be forty years since I've seen Michael,
I wonder where he is?"

"Michael who?"

"Michael Wood, the dog next door,
up the street."

"Oh," said Teddy.

"Why do you wear that bandage?" asked Teddy.

Ted looked sadly at his bandaged wrist. "Oh, just because my paw wore out," he said.

"Like my growl wore out, I suppose," suggested Teddy , glad that Ted was not perfect.

"I suppose," said Ted still searching for a clever reply. Then he had an idea.

"It gives me a worldly look," he explained.

"What does?" demanded Teddy.

"My bandage on my worn out paw," said Ted.
"With that and me together," he went on,
"I am a Worldly Bear." He remembered
that somebody once had admired him,
and shaken him, and told him he was
a worldly bear.

"What's a worldly bear?" asked Teddy.

"One that's worldly," said Ted wisely.
He was quite content just being worldly
without having to explain what it meant —
that's part of being worldly.

"I'm an Idle Bear," said Teddy.

"I know," said Ted, "You told me so."

"Don't you want to know what an Idle is?"

"No," said Ted.

"My owner is an Idle," said Teddy ignoring Ted, "so I'm an Idle too."

Ted wished he knew what an Idle was.

And he is still thinking about it.